caillou ®

and Rosie's Doll

Adapted from
the animated film:
Francine Allen
Illustration:
CINAR Animation

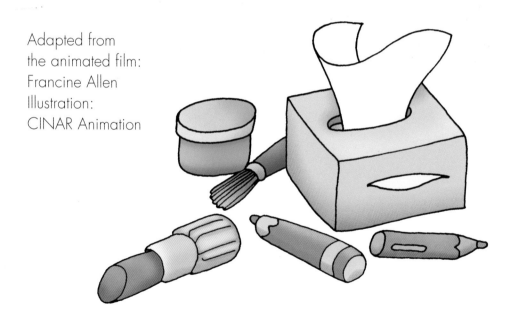

chouette CINAR ®

MW01016673

"What are you doing, Mommy?" asked Caillou.
"Putting on my makeup," she replied, carefully applying eye shadow to her eyelids.
"Why?"
"To look nice when I go out today," Mommy told him with a smile.

Caillou was very curious about all the colors Mommy was putting on her face.
He examined the many tubes and little jars on the table. "Just like my paint box!" he said to himself.

Caillou picked up a tube of lipstick.
What fun! You could make the red
lipstick inside the tube go up and
down!
"Oh, Caillou, please don't play
with that."
Reluctantly, Caillou put the tube back.
He wanted to keep playing with it.

Ding dong!
"That must be Julie," Mommy said.
"Would you let her in, Caillou, while
I finish getting ready?"
Caillou loved when Julie came to
babysit. He could hardly wait
to see her and raced to the
front door.

Now Mommy was ready to leave.
"See you later, you two! Have fun!" she said on her
way out. "Bye, Mommy!" replied Caillou and Rosie,
giving her a kiss.

Caillou and Rosie played for a long time with Julie.
They built a big house for Rosie's doll and then
they had a snack.

"Caillou, Rosie's a bit
tired. Why don't you
play by yourself now,
while I get Rosie ready
for her nap," suggested
Julie.
"Okay," replied Caillou,
picking up Rosie's doll.

As he passed Mommy's and Daddy's bedroom, Caillou noticed that all the jars and tubes of colorful makeup were still on the table. He looked at Rosie's doll and had an idea.

Caillou went to his room. He chose a few colors from his paint box and sat down on the floor with the doll. Oh! Oh! It wasn't easy tracing around the eyes and mouth…

Rosie had finally dozed off. Julie tiptoed out of the room.
All was quiet and she wondered where Caillou was.
"Caillou, where are you? Caillou... answer me!"

When Caillou heard Julie
calling, he stopped what he
was doing. He knew he was
doing something he shouldn't
and was worried that Julie
would scold him. What should
he do? Where could he hide
Rosie's doll?

"I know, in my toy box!"
Caillou ran and stuffed the doll in the chest. He barely had time
to sit down on top of it before Julie came into his room.

"Oh, there you are, Caillou," she said. "You were so quiet. What were you doing?" Caillou bit his lip. He didn't know what to say...

"Julie! Julie!" Rosie cried out suddenly.

"Oh, Rosie's crying!" said Julie. "I'll be right back."

"Caillou, do you know where Rosie's doll is?"
Julie asked, coming back into the room.
"No," replied Caillou in a very small voice.
"Are you sure? She put it down on the chair
earlier and now it's not there."
Julie spotted a doll's arm sticking out of the toy box.
"Caillou, is that Rosie's doll I see?"

Slowly, Caillou got off his toy box.

"Oh dear, Caillou. What did you do?"
sighed Julie, looking at the doll.
"I didn't do it on purpose," Caillou sobbed.

Just then, Mommy
came back from
her shopping trip.
She heard Caillou
crying.
"Uh oh, it sounds
like someone's done
something he shouldn't
have," she said,
coming into the room.

Caillou ran to his mommy. "Mommy, I didn't do it on purpose! I just wanted to play with Rosie's doll!" "I see. You didn't mean to do any harm. You were just playing?" "Yes," sobbed Caillou.

Mommy took Caillou's hand. "Come with me. We'll try to fix it."

Mommy and Caillou
filled the sink with
soapy water.
"Scrub the cheeks
and eyes really well."
Caillou scrubbed as
hard as he could, but
some of the marks
were still there.
Then Mommy tried.
"Well, that's a bit
better. Let's dry the doll
and see what Rosie
thinks of her now!"

"Look, Caillou," said Mommy. "Rosie thinks her doll looks very pretty!"
Rosie was very happy to have her doll back. She talked to it and held it close.

Caillou was relieved. He hugged Mommy. "I think my little Caillou feels a lot better now!" she said and patted Caillou's head.

© 2000 ÉDITIONS CHOUETTE (1987) INC. and CINAR CORPORATION
All rights reserved. The translation or reproduction of any excerpt of this book in any manner
whatsoever either electronically or mechanically and more specifically by photocopy and/or
microfilm is forbidden.

CAILLOU is a registered trademark of Éditions Chouette (1987) Inc.
Text adapted by Francine Allen from the scenario taken from the CAILLOU animated film series
produced by CINAR Corporation (© 1997 Caillou Productions Inc., a subsidiary of
CINAR Corporation).
All rights reserved.

Original scenario written by Matthew Cope.

We gratefully acknowledge the financial support of BPIDP, SODEC and
the Canada Council for the Arts

Canadian Cataloguing in Publication Data

Allen, Francine,1955-
Caillou and Rosie's doll
(Backpack Series)
Translation of: Caillou et la poupée.
For children aged 3 and up.
Co-published by: CINAR Corporation.

ISBN 2-89450-183-8

1. Beauty culture – Juvenile literature.   I. CINAR Corporation.
II. Title.   III. Series.

TT957.A4413 2000   j646.7'26   C00-940393-0

Printed in Hong Kong